√STO

ALLEN COUNTY PUBLIC LIBRARY
FRIENDS
3 1833 04376 0963
P9-CSF-003

# FIVE DOLLS AND THE DUKE

HELEN CLARE

# FIVE DOLLS AND THE DUKE

ILLUSTRATED BY ALIKI

PRENTICE-HALL, Inc., Englewood Cliffs, New Jersey

*Five Dolls and the Duke,* by Helen Clare

First published in the U.S.A. by Prentice-Hall, Inc., Englewood Cliffs, N.J., 1968

First published in Great Britain by The Bodley Head, 1963



*Printed in the United States of America*

Library of Congress Catalog Card Number: 68–14629
J32104

Other *FIVE DOLLS* books by Helen Clare

*FIVE DOLLS IN A HOUSE*
*FIVE DOLLS AND THE MONKEY*
*FIVE DOLLS IN THE SNOW*
*FIVE DOLLS AND THEIR FRIENDS*

*For my*
*goddaughter*
*Jane*

# CONTENTS


| | | |
|---|---|---|
| I | The Duke of Cranberry | *1* |
| II | An Earthquake | *15* |
| III | Hats to Let | *28* |
| IV | Sports Day | *43* |
| V | The Pillar-Box | *57* |
| VI | April Fools | *71* |
| VII | The Theatre | *84* |
| | Glossary | *99* |

# I

## THE DUKE OF CRANBERRY

ELIZABETH looked at the old-fashioned gentleman doll in his sedan-chair. He was very, very old indeed for he had first belonged to her great-great-grandmother, as Vanessa had. (Vanessa was the eldest of her dolls' house dolls.) The gentleman doll wore a long fawn coat with a

wide collar, and tight cream trousers. His sedan-chair was like a painted box with a pole each side to carry it by, and it had windows and a door and a padded seat inside.

This evening she had borrowed him from her granny and when she reached home the playroom was almost dark. She put on the light, and saw her dolls' house in the corner, waiting. She stood the sedan-chair down outside, turned herself small and crept in at the door. Then she heard the most delightful sound floating down from the parlour. The dolls were singing, in quiet, polite evening voices! That was Vanessa's voice, thin and quavery, and that was Jane's, as sweet as a flute. Amanda's was sharp and cheeky, Lupin's was babyish and breathy, and Jacqueline's was pointed like needles and very French.

"My feet are cold,

And I am very old!" sang the dolls, to a sad little tune. It was one of Jane's poems, Elizabeth remembered it.

"Oh, Vanessa, it sounds lovely!" she said, walking in.

Vanessa jumped up from the piano.

"Bless me, we did not hear you come, what a very late call dear landlady," she said, looking flustered.

"We were just going to bed, but now that

you've come we can stay up," said Jane, squeezing her hand.

"Let's sing Mrs. Small Jane's songs," said Amanda.

"They're lovely," Lupin added. "When I'm in bed I hear them going on in my head."

"Not only in her head, I can assure you, Mrs. Small. She sings at the top of her voice in bed, and so does Amanda."

"And then Jane often sings us to sleep," they said.

"Dear Jane is most musical," Vanessa explained, "and she has made up tunes to all her poems. I play them as best I can, but the piano needs a rest, I think, because it takes no notice and doesn't sing a single note."

"A single, tingle, wingle note," sang Amanda.

"You can play as many wrong notes as you like and no one knows," said Lupin.

"The pianna knows," said a gruff voice down the chimney, "you've broken its heart strings I dare say, playing wrong notes." It was the monkey who lived on the dolls' house roof.

"You should be in bed and asleep," Vanessa called briskly.

"I can't sleep," the monkey argued, "while there's somebody waiting to be let in. It's too interesting, it keeps me awake."

"She's not waiting to be let in," Vanessa replied, "if you mean Mrs. Small."

"I don't mean Mrs. Small, I mean a person in a kind of box."

"Box!" exclaimed the dolls.

"The box has got windows, so I can see him nodding. He's asleep. If you don't let him in quick, he'll fall off the seat, I shouldn't wonder, and break his leg and it'll be your fault."

"Goodness gracious, what is the animal talking about!" Vanessa said in alarm.

"How could anyone come in a box?" Jane said.

"You could if you were a parcel," said Lupin thoughtfully.

Vanessa walked to the stairs. "Let us all go and see, very carefully, in case it is a burglar again (we're quite used to them Mrs. Small, but they've never arrived disguised as a parcel before)." And Vanessa ran downstairs and peeped round the door. "Box indeed!" she exclaimed. "It's a sedan-chair unless I'm very much mistaken! That ignorant monkey, he's far too young and modern to know about sedan-chairs. But if it is a sedan-chair, then it's somebody of consequence calling on us, and if so, why doesn't he knock at the door?"

"Perhaps he's ashamed to have come so late," said Jane.

"Anyway he's asleep, the monkey said so," Amanda reminded them.

"If he's asleep, he can't be dangerous, so let us creep out and look," Vanessa said opening the door gently.

The dolls tiptoed out. Soon they were all round the sedan-chair, peering in at the windows each side, and whispering.

"It's a gentleman," Jane said.

"What's he doing? Lift me up!" whispered Lupin.

"I like his coat," Amanda said. "It's like that camel we once saw at the Zoo."

"He can't be a camel, as he has no hump," said Vanessa. "He's sitting quite still," she went on, "so it looks as if he *has* fallen asleep. No doubt he's very old."

"I expect his feet are cold," said Lupin quickly.

"They would be, poor gentleman. I wonder how many miles he's come?"

"Vanessa, how has he come?" said Jane.

"It's best not to enquire," said Vanessa, who always said this if anything was too hard to explain. "Though perhaps Mrs. Small knows. And where has he come from anyway?"

"Do you think he'll let me have a ride in the chair?" Amanda said eagerly.

"That depends on how badly you behave," answered Vanessa with a sniff.

"Vanessa," said Elizabeth, "don't you think we ought to ask him in?"

Vanessa glared at Elizabeth.

"What is the use," she said, "of speaking to a person who is asleep? Naturally I think we should ask him in, it would be most unmannerly and barbarous to leave him here to freeze——"

"He may have been here for hours and hours," put in Jane quickly, "because you see it gets very dark indeed in the evenings, and we go inside and put on our lights and then sometimes somebody turns on the moon, and quite suddenly it isn't dark any longer," she explained.

Elizabeth stared at Jane, thinking what it was like to be a doll.

"We know they turn it on, because we hear a click," Lupin added. "It's our lovely private moon, look."

And she pointed up to the round pearly bowl of the electric light.

"So this poor gentleman," Jane went on, "may have been here since dusk, getting frozen."

"Barbarous, barbarous, barbarous," muttered Amanda.

Lupin stood on her tiptoes and looked in at the old gentleman again.

"Perhaps he *is* frozen," she said.

"Perhaps he's fainted," said Jane.

"Perhaps he's painted," echoed Amanda.

"Of course, he's that," said Vanessa firmly, craning her head round to look more closely at the visitor. "Every proper doll is. Very nicely, too, as far as I can see, red cheeks (a little faded with age) blackish hair (a little grey) . . . . Oh!" screamed Vanessa suddenly, and she put her hand to her heart. "It's my dear Papa, the duke! The Duke of Cranberry! Come all this way from the Isle of Wight, and I did not see him arrive! How terrible to be sure, to leave my own wood and leather out here in the cold to freeze! Just think of the journey! Over the water——"

"Did he swim?" Lupin asked quickly.

"Perhaps the box floats?" Amanda said.

"Never mind all that now, we'll enquire later. Wake up, Papa. He's exhausted with the journey. Wake up, Papa!" Vanessa sang in her shrill voice. "You're here!" And she began to open the door.

"Where?" asked the duke, waking up with a start, and nearly falling off the seat.

"Here, dear Papa, you're here," Vanessa said comfortingly. "At my house."

The old gentleman blinked and rubbed his hands.

"We're delighted to welcome you. Take my arm and step out," Vanessa went on.

The duke bent himself forward, and stepped out rather stiffly.

"Well, upon my word," he began in a quavery voice, looking round at all the dolls, and up at the house, "this is a neat, modest little villa you have here, my dears, and no mistake. And who set you up here, pray?"

"Come in, come in, Papa," said Vanessa, "it's too late to stand talking in the garden——"

"Am I your Papa?" asked the gentleman, looking at Vanessa with a puzzled air.

"Certainly you are," said Vanessa crisply, "it may be many months since we met (though we visited you not so long ago at Cranberry Castle) and you may have come on a long cold journey, but there's no excuse your not remembering that." And she closed her mouth in a firm line, and pushed him towards the door.

"As you say, my dear, as you say," said the duke. "The fact is, they tell me I've lost my memory lately in patches. I had a great many children," he went on, "and I find it hard to remember."

"I am your eldest daughter Vanessa," she said.

"Capital," said he, "delighted to hear it," and he took a few hestitating steps of an old-fashioned dance in the hall.

Lupin laughed.

"Hush," said Vanessa. "This is Lupin, you remember, the youngest, you must excuse her manners, she hasn't any. Curtsey, Lupin."

Lupin did so, fell over, and giggled.

The duke giggled too, and patted her head.

"And here's Amanda," said Vanessa, "as she's pushed herself forward——"

Amanda curtsied beautifully.

"Charming, miss," said the duke nodding.

"And here's my dear Jane, the goodest and cleverest," Vanessa went on.

Jane curtsied too, very modestly and shyly. The duke twiddled his cravat and bowed.

"And this is our landlady, Mrs. Small. And this is our paying-guest," Vanessa went on, as Jacqueline performed a most graceful curtsey.

The duke bowed in all directions.

"You seem to be well provided for," he said.

"Oh, we've got lots more things! This is our kitten!" shrieked Lupin.

"And here's our parrot, come on, upstairs in the parlour," said Amanda, tugging at the duke's cuff.

"Bless my soul, most genteel," said the parrot.

The duke jumped when he heard this.

"Now sit in this chair, and toast your toes the fender," Vanessa said. She was so pleased have the duke, that her face looked redder a more polished and happier than Elizabeth h ever seen it before.

Lupin came and sat on the rug and lifted t

duke's black leather feet, one by one, on to the fender, to toast them.

"Are you hungry, Papa? That's the first thing."

The duke considered.

"Yes," he said as if he were surprised. "Excessively."

"Then what would you like?"

"Roast chicken and plum pudding. And a little port," he answered at once. "And my snuff-box."

"Splendid," said his daughter, "because roast chicken and plum pudding we always have in the house." This was true. But as they were hard and stuck to the plates, Elizabeth felt rather sorry for the hungry duke.

"As for the port, no doubt we can send out for it," Vanessa went on, darting an anxious look at Elizabeth. "Jane and you young dolls, run and fetch the things from the kitchen, we shan't trouble dear Papa to go downstairs."

There was a rush for the door, as the dolls went to collect the duke's supper. Elizabeth went too.

"What's port?" Lupin whispered.

"Red wine," Elizabeth said.

"How can we get it?" Amanda asked.

"I'll see to it."

"What's snuff?" Lupin went on.

"I think it's powdery stuff you sniff, and it makes you sneeze."

Lupin laughed. "It's nice sneezing," she said. "And fancy toasting his toes, you'd think it would hurt him."

Soon the duke sat with the flower-painted table at his elbow, on which were crammed the food and wine, a gold plate, and a knife and fork.

"'is Grace won't get fat on that," growled a voice from the chimney.

This time the duke jumped so hard that his plate went flying from his thin knees. However, as there was nothing on it, it didn't matter. Lupin picked it up and put it back.

"Who's that?" he barked.

"It's all right, Papa, it's the monkey, you remember, who lives on the roof."

"I remember no such thing," said the duke. "I told you I've lost my memory, but even if I had it, I shouldn't use it to remember a monkey."

"I agree with you entirely, Papa," Vanessa said loudly.

"Where did you lose it?" Lupin asked. "Shall I go and look?"

"Lupin is willing, but simple, Papa," Vanessa said. "Now the next question is, where is Papa going to sleep?"

"In the bath!" exclaimed Amanda, who had heard this suggested before.

"Certainly not," Vanessa said, shocked. "A barbarous suggestion."

But the duke did not seem to have heard. He was sipping his port, which was clearly much to his taste (it was crimson paint and water).

"He can have my bed," Jane said generously, "and I'll sleep in the bath, I know it fits me all right."

"It's a great pity we can't turn that paying-guest out," Vanessa said to Elizabeth, under her breath.

"You can't possibly," Elizabeth said. "But the duke should have your four-poster bed, Vanessa. And you should have Jane's room. And Jane should have Lupin's bed. And Lupin, for a great treat, can have a bed on the floor." This is the way Elizabeth herself had been turned out of her bed for a visitor.

Lupin fell for it at once.

"Oh, yes, yes, please let me, how do you do it?"

"No, me," Amanda wailed, "let me!"

"You can tomorrow. Do you agree, Vanessa?"

"It seems a perfect arrangement," Vanessa said.

So Elizabeth and Lupin and Amanda collected every cushion in the house, and with shrieks of pleasure made Lupin a bed, and piled rugs and bedspreads and cloaks and scraps to keep her warm.

"Vanessa, can I go to bed at once?" Lupin said.

"Upon my word," Vanessa answered, "this is the cleverest bed I've ever known if it makes Lupin want to go at once. Certainly you may, Lupin, we shall all go now."

"And I must go too," Elizabeth said, "it's so late."

"I'm sure you must, dear Mrs. Small, I'm surprised you haven't gone before," Vanessa said.

"Good-night!" called Elizabeth laughing. "Good-night, everybody!"

"Good-night," called the dolls.

As she went, she peeped into the sedan-chair.

"Like me juke box?" said the monkey, who had settled himself inside.

# II

## AN EARTHQUAKE

ELIZABETH's grandmother had saved her a tiny, shiny, scarlet pill-box for the dolls' house. Elizabeth sewed on a handle of red silk and there was a hat-box for Vanessa! So granny made Vanessa a new hat, round a thimble, for Vanessa's old hat with a feather was very battered.

Elizabeth wrote a label to stick on the box. It said:

*Worth: Londres: Paris*

which was the name of a famous shop. There was another, flatter pill-box which they covered with blue velvet to make a pouffe.

As she walked up to the dolls' house door, Elizabeth asked the monkey how the duke was getting on.

"Fuss, fuss, fuss," said he, "it's as bad as when that baby came. Though it's a good thing to have another man about the place. That's three, counting Hugo."

"I don't know that you can count Hugo," Elizabeth said. Hugo was the monkey's invisible friend.

Elizabeth peeped through the letter-box and knocked on the door.

"Not at home!" she heard Vanessa call.

"But you are, I can hear you," Elizabeth laughed.

"Then if you know we are at home, why knock?" Vanessa called. "But if you had proper manners you would know that 'not at home' means we are too busy to see you, and you would go away!" she finished.

"But, Vanessa, it may be Mrs. Small," said Jane's voice anxiously.

"It is Mrs. Small," screamed Lupin.

"Come in, dear landlady," sang Vanessa trying to change to a friendly voice and not doing it very well. "We are so extremely busy, and I thought you were the dustman, so I decided to try saying not at home, though I'm not surprised it didn't work for of course it's a lie," she whispered. "Now the strange thing is Papa arrived with absolutely no luggage at all, and he cannot remember why. (His memory is not as good as it was.) I quite expect that idle man-servant of his was too lazy to pack. Or else, of course, his box fell out, coming over the water——"

"But if the box had fallen out, he'd have fallen out, too," Amanda said.

"Not necessarily. Anyway, Papa's very good wood, he'd float. The fact remains he has *nothing,* so we're very busy making do and pretending, as we always say."

The duke sat with his feet on the fender, nodding and smiling. On his head was a night-cap, knitted by Amanda.

"How de do, how de do," he said to Elizabeth.

"Good morning, your Grace," said she. "I hope you're quite well after your long journey."

"Capital, fit as a fiddle," said he, nodding the very long night-cap.

"I went on too long," said Amanda. "I like doing it."

"It's better than not long enough," Vanessa said, "but he doesn't need it on now." And she whipped it off.

"I was cold about the ears," said the duke.

"You should have drawn the curtains," suggested Elizabeth.

"Ah. Clever woman, your landlady," said the duke to his daughter. "Why didn't we think of that?"

"Because we were asleep," Vanessa said at once.

"Has he got curtains for his *ears*?" whispered Lupin. And Amanda giggled.

"Come, Lupin, Mrs. Small means the bed curtains," Vanessa said.

"Now here are his handkerchiefs," said Jane, who had stitched some tiny squares of silk.

"I'm much obleeged, miss," the duke said.

"And, Vanessa," Elizabeth announced, "I've brought something for Papa too—I mean the duke." And she ran downstairs to fetch the pouffe.

"Oh, a footstool!" said Jane.

"How very useful indeed!"

"It's a pouffe," Elizabeth explained.

"Don't let Papa hear you say 'poof'!" Vanessa whispered. "It's very vulgar."

"It's French," Elizabeth said.

"It would be," said Vanessa venomously, looking at poor Jacqueline. But she only smiled sweetly and patted the pouffe.

"French for what?" said Lupin.

"For a tuffet, like this, to sit on."

"Like little Miss Muffet, no doubt. We hope there'll be no spiders. Get off, Lupin, dear Papa shall put his feet on it. Many thanks indeed, kind landlady."

"And this, Vanessa," Elizabeth said, bringing in the hat-box, "this is for you! Because you always wear a hat."

Vanessa opened her mouth, and then her arms, and hugged the scarlet hat-box to her wooden chest. Her cheeks went very red, and she looked almost as if she were going to cry.

"Oh, Mrs. Small, how exceedingly kind! I have always wanted a scarlet hat-box! I do thank you a thousand times——"

"Vanessa, you'll never count up to a thousand!" exclaimed Lupin.

"Open it, Vanessa!"

Vanessa knelt on the carpet and opened the hat-box. Under the tissue paper was the little grey satin thimble-shaped hat that granny had made. Vanessa lifted it out, and put it on at once, tossing her old hat away. (Lupin picked it up.)

"Oh!" said Jane. "How smart!"

"Does it suit me?" Vanessa said to her father.

"I protest I never saw anything more elegant," said he, tapping his toe.

"But don't throw away this hat with a feather will you, Vanessa?" Lupin said anxiously. "Because I'm used to it."

"No. I shall keep it for everyday," Vanessa said.

"Then when will you wear the new one?" demanded Lupin.

Vanessa sighed.

"Lupin, you take too much explaining to," she said.

And Vanessa never explained, for then the most extraordinary things began to happen.

The room grew rather dark, as if there were a great cloud in the back garden. Then there was a sudden jerk which knocked the more upright dolls like Vanessa and Jane on to their knees. Lupin and Amanda and Jacqueline, who were stooping down to look at the hat-box, fell right over on to their heads and laughed, and the duke slid off his chair.

"Gracious heavens! It's no laughing matter, you silly dolls! Whatever is happening?" Vanessa said scrambling up, and rushing to help her father.

"I think it was an earthquake," said Jane, "but it's finished."

"I think it's a thunderstorm coming," said Amanda. "Look how dark it is!"

Then there was another jerk, followed by a long, loud swishing noise. It felt to Elizabeth as if the house were moving.

Swish, jerk. Swish, jerk. Swish, jerk.

"What shall we do, Vanessa?" Lupin wailed.

"There's too much noise to do anything," Vanessa said, clutching her Papa. The house was full of bumps and judders as things fell over at each jerk. In the kitchen, there were clatters and bangs and tinny noises.

"It's the pots and pans," Amanda said.

In the dining-room, where Elizabeth had staggered to look, all the little gold plates and candlesticks were dancing a jig on the table and the mantelshelf.

There was another jerk, and a tremendous crash from the hall.

"Vanessa, Jane," called Lupin in a shocked voice, "grandfather's fallen over on his face!"

"Leave him where he is, he'll be all right," Elizabeth said, looking at the clock. "It's safer."

"Vanessa, the front lawn's all rolled up," Amanda screamed, staring from the parlour window. "It looks so funny."

"Rolled up?" said Vanessa faintly. "Then it *must* be an earthquake! Fetch me my smelling-salts, Jane, before I faint."

"You needn't faint, Vanessa," Amanda called, "we're just going along. Like in the train. It's fun. I can see that castle getting nearer."

This was too much for Vanessa. She stopped fainting and looked cross.

"Houses don't go along," she said firmly. "I never heard of anything so absurd. What do you say, Papa?"

"Madness! Absolute madness," said the duke.

"Houses do move sometimes," Elizabeth said, holding on to the piano. For she had realized what was happening. She and Edward, her brother, had talked of moving the dolls' house. Now Edward was suddenly doing it, without any warning. "In America, they put them on trailers, and wheel them along."

"We are NOT in America," said Vanessa.

Lupin ran in. "Where's the kitten?" she said. "Oh, supposing he's outside, he may be run over. Vanessa, can I go out and get him?"

"No. You may be run over yourself. If we really are going along, as Amanda says. The kitten must take his chance."

"Where's Jacqueline?" Elizabeth asked.

"She's right in her bed, under the covers," Lupin said.

"For once I don't blame her, though it is very cowardly."

Swish. Jerk. Crash. Jingle.

And the parrot's cage fell over.

"Not 'alf, not 'alf, not 'alf," he said in a muffled voice. "Children half price."

"Bless me, the bird's demented, and I don't wonder. Help Mrs. Small, Lupin. What a good thing we weren't drinking tea, we should all have been scalded!" Vanessa said breathlessly.

Elizabeth and Lupin lifted up the parrot's cage between them.

"Bless my soul, most genteel," he said.

"That's exactly what it is not," Vanessa retorted. "It's the most dangerous way of moving house I've ever heard of. Why it's we who should do the moving, not the house! And where is Jane?"

"Comforting Robin, and holding the cradle," Lupin reported. "I nearly fell downstairs, coming down."

"I say, what about the monkey?" Amanda said. "I hope he doesn't fall off."

"And I quite hope he does."

"You are mean, Vanessa."

There was another long, tremendous swish, and then a strange feeling as if you were on a roundabout (Edward was turning the house round) when lots more things fell over, and the dolls all screamed.

And then at last there was silence. It grew light

again, as the shadow of Edward left the windows. Nobody spoke. Elizabeth hardly dared to breathe.

"I think we're there!" announced Amanda triumphantly, from the window. "Because everything's standing still again!"

"The question is, where?" said Vanessa. "*Where* are we? We may never find out."

"But I can see our garden in the distance!" Amanda screamed. "And the stable, and all the things. So we can't be far away."

"Vanessa," said Lupin. "The horses! We can't leave them, who'll look after them?"

"Robin was as good as gold," said Jane coming in, carrying him, "and I didn't even have to rock the cradle."

"I should think not indeed, there was enough rocking without that. Now, Mrs. Small, what do you suggest about all our possessions left behind? What a mercy we weren't in the garden, we should be homeless refugees by now, left behind!"

"We'll all go back and load up the trap and fetch them," Elizabeth said.

"Hooray!" said Lupin and Amanda.

So this is what they did.

When at last they reached the stable, Lupin harnessed the mice, who were upset by the earthquake and very frisky, Amanda held the trap, and Elizabeth, Jane and Vanessa loaded in all the things, including the kitten, who crept out of the stable, to Lupin's joy and relief. As for the paying-guest she was evidently still under the bedclothes, for she had not come with them.

"Where are the horses going tonight?" Lupin asked as they got ready to go. "Can they come in with us?"

"They must stay in the new garden. No horses in the house. We must draw the line somewhere," Vanessa said.

"They'll never stay behind a line," Lupin announced. And Elizabeth laughed.

They were just about to drive off when who should stroll up but the monkey.

"Hooray!" said Amanda.

"Come to fetch 'is Grace's box," he said.

Vanessa stared.

"Where have you been? What happened? What were you doing when the house moved?" she said, as if it were all his fault.

"I was not at home," he replied in a lordly way.

While Vanessa was thinking what to say to this, Amanda shouted:

"Please, please can I ride in the duke's box?"

"Very well," Vanessa said, and she climbed into the trap and whipped up the mice. Meanwhile the monkey and Elizabeth picked up the chair, with Amanda bouncing on the seat, and the procession started. Past miles of dull wall they went, past Elizabeth's post-office, past Edward's castle, until at last they reached their new house.

"Only it's the same house," said Jane with great satisfaction. "I'm so glad, I liked it as it was."

"And yet somehow it seems a bit new, doesn't it?" Lupin said, waving to the duke, who was at the window with Jacqueline.

"Of course, it's looking another way," said Vanessa, "which might make it seem new."

"Houses can't look," argued Amanda.

"Indeed they can, what are their windows for?" Vanessa retorted. "What is more," she went on mysteriously, as they began to unload the trap, "it appears that they can also walk."

And she stumped into the house, the black velvet kitten wriggling under her arm.

# III

## HATS TO LET

THE dolls' house was used to its new place, and looked as if it had been there for ever. Elizabeth had brought over the velvet grass and the fence and had even added a scarlet pillar-box, in the road outside. (It was really a money-box.)

From the gate she saw a little white paper flag

stuck in the green velvet by its pin. She hurried up to it, expecting it to say:

*Keep off the Grass*

But instead of this it said:

*Hats to Let*

Elizabeth laughed out loud. The monkey, who was watching her, called out curiously:

"What's the joke? It's rude to laugh."

"They must mean flats to let."

"They do not. They means what they sez. I can hear them at it, hatting and chatting."

Elizabeth walked in at the door and called out, "Vanessa! Can I come in?"

"Come in, come upstairs, Mrs. Small, I'm most anxious to see you," she heard, in Vanessa's shrill voice, "because that monkey's been saying that if we open a shop, you'll charge more rent."

"I won't," Elizabeth said at once. "You ought to know that by now. What are you doing?"

The room was scattered with pretty scraps, and piled all round the duke on the sofa were lots of things which looked (a little) like–hats.

"Mrs. Small," said Jane, with pins in her mouth, "it's so lovely, we're going to have a hat shop!"

"We've never had a shop before," squealed Lupin.

"I've made six," shouted Amanda.

"Each worse than the last," teased the duke.

*"Voilà,"* said Jacqueline, holding up a hat like a lampshade, "we hold *un boutique,* Mrs. Small."

"She will keep calling it a booteek, it's nothing whatever to do with bootees, this isn't a baby shop," Vanessa whispered, crossly.

"I expect it's French for this kind of shop," said Elizabeth. "Fancy your letting them have a shop!" she added.

"That's just what I thought," remarked Vanessa, with surprise. "But they were so set upon it, no doubt it was my new hat which gave them the idea, and surely hats is more genteel than groceries (which Lupin wanted because she likes weighing things) or sweets (which the paying-guest wanted for the reason you know) ." (Jacqueline was rather a greedy doll.)

"How do you do it?" said Elizabeth, going over to look at the hats. "You must have taken hours!"

"It's simple, once you have the crown," Jane explained.

"Do you know what the crown is?" shouted Lupin. "It just means the top of your head! Not a king's crown at all!"

"Jack fell down and broke his crown!" Vanessa sang, in a wobbly voice and very high.

"But I've made a *proper* crown, look, with five points," Lupin said. "In case the Queen comes," she whispered.

It was made from a piece of gold foil.

"Of course, we don't expect Her Majesty at our humble shop, even though it is to be a select, model, hat shop, but it gave Lupin pleasure," Vanessa said. "These gold and silver things are excellent for the crowns," she went on. "You simply bend them round whatever shape you want——"

Elizabeth saw that they were milk bottle tops.

Cover them with stuff——" shouted Amanda.

"And decorate them with flowers or feathers or ribbons!" finished Jane.

"And they're *not* models, Vanessa, they're real," Amanda added.

"Ignorant doll, she doesn't know what model hat shop means. Mrs. Small knows, I'll be bound," Vanessa said, sewing at a plant-pot shaped hat in red silk.

"I think model means when every hat is different," Elizabeth said.

"Just so," Vanessa agreed. "Hand-made and different."

"Oh, I must do one," said Elizabeth, as eager as the rest.

"Do, do Mrs. Small. Choose some nice shape,

that is fashionable. The house is full of them. Christmas puddings, saucepans, plant-pots, basins, lampshades, even our own heads. Papa's head has been most useful, he sits so still," Vanessa whispered.

"I'll do it round my own head," Elizabeth said. And she pressed a milk bottle top on, to fit.

"Now you cut off what's too big," said Jane, giving her the huge scissors.

Elizabeth peered into the mirror, and shaped herself a model hat.

"Vanessa!" wailed Lupin from the hall.

Everybody ran out to see what Lupin was doing. She had made a crimson velvet tammy round the top of the stair-post and now she was tugging and pushing to get it off.

"You ridiculous doll, you should have taken it off before you sewed it. Now you will have to cut the stitches and do it again," Vanessa said.

"It can stay there," Lupin announced sulkily.

"It can not. I won't have the stair-post given a hat, it will get conceited. And anyway, gentlemen don't keep their hats on in the house. Ask Papa."

"I'll help you, Lupin," Jane said.

"And everybody hurry up, and finish the hat she is doing. Before we know where we are the customers will be arriving," Vanessa said.

"We do know where we are," said Amanda, cheekily.

"I'm afraid nobody will come," whispered Jane to Elizabeth. "How will they know it's a hat shop? Vanessa says we can't have a notice——"

"Certainly not. Most vulgar," Vanessa agreed. "Such ladies as we all are. His Grace would order his chair and leave at once."

"But there is a notice!" Elizabeth said, remembering. "It says Hats to Let."

Vanessa stared at Elizabeth with her mouth open.

"That's not what it ought to say," she remarked at last, "if it says anything."

"No, because you don't let them do you, you sell them," Elizabeth agreed.

"We hope so," Vanessa said firmly.

"You don't, you let people have them," said Amanda, running downstairs, "and when they've had them they let you have them back."

The duke laughed a crackly laugh.

"And what do you know about it, pray?" he asked.

"Everything. Me and the monkey put up the notice. And I want my hats back," Amanda pouted.

"Nonsense!" Vanessa said. "You'll ruin the business before you start. It's the most ridiculous notice. It's houses that are to let——"

"Yes. *Flats* to let," said Elizabeth.

"I don't know what flats are, to be sure, but——" 

"They're half of houses. Or even a third or quarter of houses," Elizabeth explained.

Vanessa stared again.

"What a ridiculous notion," she said. "Whoever heard of houses being cut in pieces. Why, supposing you only got the kitchen half, it would be most uncomfortable and absurd. Where would you go to bed?"

"In the cupboard," said Lupin at once. "The rice does. And bath in the sink."

"A barbarous suggestion. Now, what shall we do, Mrs. Small, to attract the customers?"

"Put some hats in the window," said Elizabeth at once. "I'll show you."

Vanessa looked very doubtful, but she was soon arranging hats with the others.

"Now, some paper and a pencil for the bills. And what about the money?"

"The customers will bring their own money," Vanessa said. "No money, no hat."

"But we must have some change."

"Lupin, go and get the rent from the tea-pot," said Vanessa. (For the dolls always used cough drops for money and kept them in the tea-pot.)

"Now the prices," said Jane. "Quickly, before anyone comes."

"Children half price!" put in the parrot.

"Listen to that bird, he's really quite quick," Vanessa said. "He recognizes words he knows."

Elizabeth picked up a pink net hat made by Jane.

"This can be eighty-four and eleven," she said.

"Eighty-four and eleven!" echoed Vanessa. "What a very old hat, nearly eighty-five."

Elizabeth shrieked with laughter. But Jane understood.

"It means shillings and pence," she said writing. And Vanessa blushed, and stamped round the room.

"And this rotten old thing's worth nothing," Amanda said, picking up the first hat she had made. "Put nothing, Jane, on the label."

"Oh, no," said Jane wisely, "nobody'll want it if you say 'nothing'. Shall I say 'free'?"

"Then everyone will want it, and there'll be a fight," Vanessa stated.

"What about the two in the window?" Lupin asked.

"You never have the price on in the window, it's not at all genteel," Vanessa said. "You lure people in, to ask how much, and then they find it hard to escape," she explained. "And what about wrapping them up?" she added.

"I shall wear mine," Amanda said.

"I want a scarlet hat-box," said Lupin, slyly.

"We'll just have to use tissue-paper," Elizabeth decided.

At last they were ready.

"I'm going to be the first customer," whispered Elizabeth, "as it's really your shop."

And she walked into the parlour as if she were some grand stranger.

"Good-morning, madam," Vanessa began, smiling sweetly.

"Good-afternoon," said Elizabeth also smiling, but in a high and mighty way.

"Well, make up yer minds," said the monkey's voice, down the chimney. "Why not have good-night for a change?"

Vanessa looked cross but took no notice. "And can I show madam a hat?" she went on.

"She can see 'em for 'erself," said the voice again. "Dozens of 'em."

"I suppose that's your shop detective?" said Elizabeth quickly. "In case anyone steals the hats?"

"Just so, madam," said Vanessa, looking surprised, but catching the idea. "He's well hidden, isn't he. Under the counter. Now what shape had you in mind?"

"I like that big, round blue one," Elizabeth said. And she pointed to one Lupin had made. Lupin was very pleased.

"I did it round a saucepan," she whispered.

"Oh, hush," said Vanessa, under her breath as she put the hat on Elizabeth. "Most fashionable, it suits madam very well," she said aloud.

But Elizabeth had completely disappeared.

"I can't see out," she said, trying not to laugh. "So it doesn't suit me at all."

"It was the largest saucepan," Lupin put in, rather crest-fallen.

"Excellent as a disguise, madam," Vanessa said, patting it.

"But I don't want a disguise," wailed the customer, "and I can't see." Amanda giggled and giggled, and even Jane smiled.

"Vanessa, there's a hole where the handle was, turn it round, she can see out of that!" said Lupin.

Vanessa did so.

"There. How's that, madam?"

"It's like a knight in armour," Elizabeth said, one eye peering through the hole. She could see the duke, who winked at her.

"There's no need to wear it at night, madam," Vanessa explained.

There was a smothered laugh from inside.

"And I can't even laugh in it. No, I won't have it," said Elizabeth taking it off. "I'll try that red one instead."

The red plant-pot fitted excellently. Jane wrapped it in paper, Lupin wrote out a bill with her finger for fifty-two and twelvepence, Elizabeth paid her money, and was given some very sticky change by Jacqueline.

"And excuse my saying so, but your assistants shouldn't suck the change," Elizabeth said, as she sailed out, meeting Amanda on the landing.

"Good evening, madam," said Vanessa, "and what can I show you?"

"I want that one and that one and that one, please," Amanda said, too busy to be polite, and picking up her three favourite hats. One of them was Lupin's favourite, too.

"You can't have that one," she said, snatching the little blue velvet one, "I made it specially to go with my vest! Vanessa, she can't have it," Lupin wailed.

"Your turn next, don't be rude to the customers, remember there's a duke present; and also you don't wear a hat with a vest," said Vanessa anxiously, "not if you're well dressed." But Lupin never was, as she usually wore a vest and nothing else.

She and Amanda were by now fighting, and hats were flying in all directions. Meanwhile Jacqueline took the chance to buy the most expensive hat in the shop, and poor Jane who had made it and wanted it herself, had to pretend she didn't mind. Vanessa suddenly became a customer, and tried everything on in turn, and sometimes two at once; and Elizabeth ran back to help serve.

"And what can I show you, sir?" she asked his Grace.

"I want a deer-stalker my dear," said he.

"There's nothing cheap in this shop, your Grace," Vanessa said, "and there aren't any stalkers expensive or otherwise."

"What *is* a stalker?" said Lupin. And she stopped fighting Amanda at once.

"A *deer*-stalker," said the duke.

"I've heard of a flower stalk, but not a deer stalk," said Amanda. "What is it?"

"You wear it to go stalking deer in," explained Elizabeth.

"Deer don't *have* stalks," Vanessa finished crossly, feeling very muddled, "and we don't have stalkers. So try again Papa, I mean your Grace."

Into the middle of this argument walked a large figure in a long cloak. He slammed the door, to make himself noticed, and then coughed. Vanessa swung round from the mirror.

"All shop detectives to stay under the counter," she said firmly.

"Oh, let him come, Vanessa," said Amanda.

"Ladies' hats only," repeated Vanessa.

"Oh, do let him play," begged Lupin.

Vanessa smiled a little stiffly, and gave in.

"Well, sir?" she said.

"Very, thanks," he replied. Amanda and Elizabeth laughed and clapped.

"It's clear you've never been shopping before," Vanessa muttered behind her hand. "You don't even know the words." Then she tried again.

"Yes, sir?" she managed to say. "What would you like?"

"Got any bowlers?" said the monkey.

There was silence for a minute, and then Amanda said: "This is a bowler, Vanessa, it must be, because I did it round a bowl."

"Can't abide mauve," said the monkey, putting it on, "and anyway it's too small."

"Mauve certainly doesn't suit a ginger complexion," Vanessa replied with a nasty sniff.

"What about that busby?" he said, picking up a tall fur hat.

"Does it buzz?" Lupin asked with interest.

"Not all the time," whispered Vanessa. "Well it might be worse, sir," she added.

"What I really want," he went on, picking over the hats, "is a topper. Top people wear top hats."

Vanessa forgot her shop manners altogether at this. "You're not a top person," she said spitefully, "so you needn't think it. And how you dare suggest it in the presence of the Duke of Cranberry I don't know."

"I am," argued the monkey. "I live on top of the roof. What could be topper than that?"

There was really no answer to this, so Vanessa quickly decided to close the shop.

"Closing-time!" she sang out. "All customers to leave the premises or they'll be put away with the goods. Jane, help me tidy up, Amanda count the money, without eating it, Lupin pile up the hats, Mrs. Small lock the door, nobody fall over the duke," she said, bustling about.

"Some shop," said the monkey, taking his busby and bounding downstairs. "All the same, I likes this one," he said to Elizabeth, as he swung back on to the roof again. And he pressed it on over his ears, and stood to attention by the chimney, like a sentry outside the palace.

"So do I, it suits your nice ginger complexion very well indeed," Elizabeth called.

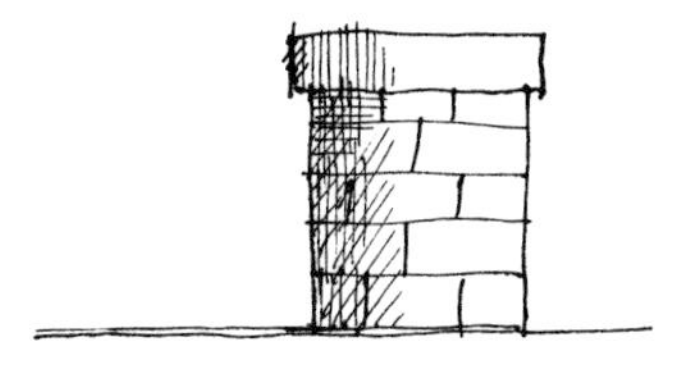

# IV

## SPORTS DAY

EDWARD had made the dolls' house a swing. The frame and the seat were wooden, and the ropes were of best string. He nailed the feet of the frame to the floor through the green velvet of the dolls' front garden, and as soon as he had gone Elizabeth hurried up to the door, eager to show it to them.

It was then that she heard shouts and screams of excitement, and one voice, louder than the rest, which sounded like Vanessa's, calling:

"Ready, steady, go!"

Next there was a sound of breathless giggling, and Elizabeth hurried round the house in time to see all the dolls crawling as fast as they could over the green lawn towards a tape. They were evidently having a race. It was a red tape (which was really her dressing-gown cord) and it was held at one end by the monkey and at the other by the parrot, in his beak. Jane was having a hard time with her long green nightdress, and Vanessa's hat (the old one) had fallen over her eyes.

Meanwhile the duke sat in a deck-chair, his legs straight out in front, calling: "Bravo, bravo," in a shrill quavery voice.

"Oh, you do look funny!" Elizabeth shouted, laughing. All the dolls jumped up from the race and ran towards her, and the parrot dropped the tape in order to say:

"Children half price. Ready steady go. Children half ready!"

"Nonsense! Hark at that bird," Vanessa said breathlessly. "Half ready, indeed, we're quite ready, except perhaps for Lupin, who is certainly a child. Dear Mrs. Small, we're having a sports day! To entertain Papa and amuse the young ones!"

"There are hundreds of races, it's *such* fun, that was only the first," Amanda screamed.

"Vanessa says she's got a whole list in her head," Lupin said, dancing round. "Will you go in for them?"

"Do, do, Mrs. Small," said Jane, who looked very pink. "Six is better than five."

"And one is better than none," Vanessa added. "At least, in most cases, though not in the case of that monkey," she whispered.

"And three is better than me," suggested Lupin modestly, not understanding.

"And two is better than you," screamed Amanda, pointing at Vanessa.

"You're too excited, Amanda," said Vanessa.

Jacqueline smiled at Elizabeth and twirled round on her toe.

"She's showing off," Vanessa said. "I told her she need not come, as the French are no good at races, anyway not at English ones——"

"Vanessa, it's a wonder she stays here at all," Elizabeth said sternly. "You're most unkind to her whenever you get the chance."

"I wish I got more chances," said Vanessa, with spirit, "but they're all wasted as she doesn't understand. However, it's always easier to be rude to someone who doesn't understand, you can say whatever you please. Form up, everybody, at the starting line. *Behind* the line, Lupin, not in front of it. Lupin likes to cheat," Vanessa whispered to Eizabeth, "but it's really because she scarcely knows what behind and in front mean."

"It's her wot cheats," called the monkey, *"she* says ready steady go and she's gone before she says it."

"Oh, *Vanessa,"* said Elizabeth in a shocked voice. (But she had often done it herself.)

"It's not true," said Vanessa. "You should know better, Mrs. Small, than to listen to a word he says."

"It is a tiny bit true," Lupin put in. "I saw you." Vanessa blushed.

"The starter shouldn't be in the race," Elizabeth explained. "Couldn't the monkey be starter?"

"Certainly not, Mrs. Small——" Vanessa began. "I don't trust him an inch——"

"But it's we who have to be trusted," Elizabeth said.

"Not to walk an inch over the line," explained Jane.

"Very well, but I dare say he'll get it wrong," Vanessa said sulkily.

"Now come on," Elizabeth called, getting ready. The line, she noticed, was a white chalk one, on the green velvet. It was not very straight, so that some dolls were further forward than others. But you must draw the line somewhere, she said to herself, smiling.

"Let's have a flat race next," she suggested.

"Flat on our fronts or flat on our backs?" said Lupin.

"Flat on our feet, perhaps," said Amanda.

"Flat feet are not at all good, so I've always heard," Vanessa remarked.

"It just means a running race," Elizabeth explained laughing.

"Then it should say what it means. Come along, all. Ready, steady, oh, I forgot."

"Come on, Monkey," ordered Elizabeth.

The monkey stood to attention and pulled the tape taut and the parrot flapped his wings. Then the velvet kitten wandered on to the grass in front of the race.

"Get off the course," roared Vanessa, waving her arms. But the black velvet kitten simply lay on his back with his paws in the air.

"Puss, puss!" called the duke.

"He'll get stamped on," said Lupin.

"That's his affair," sniffed Vanessa.

"Oh, come on," said Amanda.

"*Vite!*" said Jacqueline.

"She means feet," Vanessa said. "Hers are over the line no doubt."

"Ready," roared the monkey. Everybody crouched, being ready. "Steady," he said. "DON'T go," he finished loudly and hugged himself with mischief.

The result was a muddle. Some started, some did not, and some went back, and bumped into the others.

The duke stretched his legs in the air and laughed, and Vanessa stamped her wooden foot in a fury.

"Ha ha, muddled you up that time," the monkey laughed, dancing up and down.

"I told you what would happen, Mrs. Small," Vanessa stormed, "if you let him do it."

"All right," said Elizabeth. "We'll let the duke do it. Will you say go, your Grace?" she asked.

"Go," said the duke absent-mindedly.

Vanessa sighed.

"Not *yet*, Papa," she explained, "but when we're all ready."

Elizabeth won the running race (which was not surprising as she had proper legs) . Vanessa looked rather cross at this and announced:

"Blind race, next. Come along, all tie up your eyes. And *don't* use that stuff you can see through, it's cheating."

"It's not, it's nylon," the monkey said.

This was the oddest race Elizabeth had ever heard of. Perhaps Vanessa was thinking of blind-man's-buff? But the dolls seemed quite happy and all dived for the scrapbox, and tied each other up.

"Now I don't know where the line is!" wailed Lupin.

"Nor do I," said Amanda giggling.

"Shall I peep?" said Jane.

"Yes, yes," said Jacqueline.

Elizabeth wisely led them all to the line before she tied her own eyes up, and then the race started. But the dolls ran in all directions, bumped into each other and turned round in circles. When they were in a scrum in the middle, the monkey ran round with his red tape and tied them up into a blind bunch with the parrot.

"Let us out!" Vanessa screamed, stamping.

"Hoit-y-toit-y," said the duke helpless with laughter.

"I'm squashed," said Lupin.

"Anyway, who's won?" asked Elizabeth.

"Nobody," said the monkey solemnly. "It's a tie!"

"Well, untie it at ONCE," Vanessa ordered.

The monkey sadly obeyed and Vanessa

stumped off across the grass.

"What's next, Vanessa?" Lupin said.

Vanessa thought a minute.

"Egg-and-bacon race," she replied.

Elizabeth shrieked.

"You mean egg-and-spoon race."

"I mean egg-and-bacon race, Mrs. Small, one person is the egg, and the other is the bacon, and you tie them together, since egg and bacon always go together, as everyone knows——"

"That's three-legged race," Elizabeth argued.

"Not when *I* was at school," said Vanessa sternly. "Come along, Lupin, you're obviously an egg, I'll be your bacon." And she began to tie her leg to Lupin's.

"You mean leg-and-bacon race," Lupin said.

"If anybody else argues about what I mean——" Vanessa began, crossly.

"Come on, Jane, we'll go together," Elizabeth whispered.

This left Amanda and Jacqueline, and since Amanda tied them up with Jacqueline facing backwards, they did not stand much chance. "*Au secours!*" screamed Jacqueline being dragged along backwards.

"That's another race altogether, we'll have that next," Vanessa called. "Backwards race."

Fortunately she forgot about this one, for when Jane and Elizabeth had won the egg-and-bacon race, Vanessa said, looking hard at Elizabeth:

"Nobody is allowed more than two prizes."

"What's next, what's next?" Lupin said.

"Slow race," Vanessa said. "Quite simple, just as slow as you can."

"Ready, steady, go," said the duke.

Nobody moved an inch.

"Ready, steady, go," he said again.

But all the dolls stood like statues. So Elizabeth quickly made a new rule.

"Everybody to keep moving a little all the time," she said.

"Landladies not allowed to make rules," Vanessa answered, looking the other way.

"Mrs. Small's right," Jane said, "we'll never end if we don't begin." And she began to move a tiny bit on her pointy feet. The rest followed.

But the monkey got tired of waiting and started to skip with the tape; and Vanessa said crossly:

"A ridiculous race, I cannot think who made it up."

"You did," said Amanda.

"Now, Mrs. Small," Vanessa said, taking no notice, "what other races are there?"

Elizabeth thought hard.

"There's sack race," she began.

"We're not sacks," Vanessa said firmly.

"Or there's parents' race," Elizabeth added.

"We're not parents. Except for Papa and he can't run it on his own."

Elizabeth agreed.

"Then there's wheelbarrow race."

"There's only one wheelbarrow, and that's Robin's pram," said Jane.

"No, *we* have to be the wheelbarrows," said Elizabeth.

"A barbarous suggestion," replied Vanessa. "I for one will never be a wheelbarrow. How do you do it?" she added with interest.

"I pick up your ankles and you run along on your hands."

"Oh, yes, let's, Vanessa!" said Amanda.

"Certainly not, we shall break peoples' wrists," Vanessa said. Elizabeth agreed that they might.

"Then there's obstacle race," she said.

"And what is that, pray?"

"You have the whole course full of things to jump over or climb through or crawl under, they're the obstacles you see——"

But just then, Lupin, who had got very tired of the slow race and run away, came rushing round from the front garden.

"Vanessa, Vanessa, there's a new thing in the

front garden, do come and see, I think you're meant to sit on it——"

The dolls forgot sports day and ran helter-skelter to the front, the duke hobbling after them.

"Look! A sort of chair on ropes!" Lupin said.

"You sillies, don't you know what it is? It's a swing, I've had it made for you! Look, I'll show you."

And Elizabeth sat on the little swing and began to work herself up.

"Give me a push, Monkey," she called.

The monkey gladly did so, and soon Elizabeth was going as high as she could.

"Oh, oh!" said Lupin and Amanda and Jacqueline.

"How do you get down again?" asked Jane.

"Don't fly away, whatever happens," Vanessa said.

Elizabeth slowed down and jumped off.

"Now, Lupin, you go first," she said, "as you found it."

All the rest helped Lupin on. She clutched the string, the monkey pushed, and with shrill screams she flew higher and higher, while the other dolls clapped and laughed. And then an astonishing thing happened. The monkey gave a tremendous push, Lupin flew forwards, lost her hold, and sailed off the swing. She flew right over the house and out of sight.

"Oh, how terrible," Jane said, "poor Lupin!"

"It's your fault, Monkey, you pushed too hard," said Elizabeth.

"What an exceedingly dangerous sport," said Vanessa, "but it looked rather nice to do," she added, running round to the back lawn. "What a good thing it was Lupin, she can come to no harm, she's only cotton, you know," she whispered to Elizabeth.

And there was Lupin, sitting on the velvet, breathless, with her eyebrows higher than ever.

"Bless my soul! Clean over the house! Well done, Lupin, there's no question who won the obstacle race, Mrs. Small, is there, and that's Lupin. Stand up and let's feel you. Not that she's likely to have any bones broken, as she's not the bony sort," Vanessa finished.

"Oh, it was lovely," Lupin said recovering her voice at last.

And they all ran back to the swing and quarrelled to get on it.

That's a good thing, Elizabeth thought, we shan't even have to think of any prizes. "Good-bye, Vanessa!" she called. "I'm glad you like it! I enjoyed sports day!"

"Good-bye, good-bye," called the dolls, busy

watching Amanda on the swing.

The monkey roared as he pushed, and Jane and Jacqueline stood each side, their heads going backwards and forwards as Amanda passed. It was clear that Amanda was going to try to fly over the roof, too. The duke held Lupin's hand and muttered:

"Madness! Absolute madness."

And Vanessa called, "Many thanks, kind Mrs. Small, it's a splendid diversion!"

So Elizabeth slipped away and left them to it.

(And don't you try doing what Lupin did, for only dolls can do it safely.)

# V

## THE PILLAR-BOX

ELIZABETH was going up the dolls' house path one day, when the door opened and Lupin and Amanda rushed out to meet her.

"Oh, Mrs. Small, wait for us, we've just got to catch the post," Amanda shouted, her arms full of letters. "Vanessa says it may go!"

But Lupin stopped and whispered, "Does she mean the pillar-box will go, Mrs. Small, like the house did? Because I've watched from the window for hours and hours and it hasn't moved at all."

"Ridiculous doll," called Vanessa from the hall, "it's the letters that go: a postman comes and takes them. Not that they ever do go," Vanessa whispered, "but we live in hopes. Lupin discovered this convenient pillar-box, Mrs. Small, so while we've got it we're using it. You never know when it may disappear."

Elizabeth had not thought about emptying the box at all.

"Don't bend them Lupin, you careless doll!" Vanessa called, as she saw Lupin, lifted up by Amanda, stuffing a bundle of letters into the box.

Lupin put her arm right in.

"I can feel them, Vanessa!" she yelled. "Millions of letters. I can stir them up."

"It's no good stirring *them* up," Vanessa retorted. "We need to stir the post people up. What is the use, Mrs. Small, of having a letter-box if the letters are never collected? Why it's preposterous."

"Preposterous, pre-post-erous!" hissed Amanda who liked this new word of Vanessa's.

"Perhaps the postman's ill," said Elizabeth.

"Then they should send another. Come in,

dear Mrs. Small, we're delighted to see you, one must have a rest from writing letters some time," and she led Elizabeth into the dining-room.

"I'm not having a rest, I'm going to do some more for the next post," Lupin said. "I'm going to cram it so full, that there's no more room!"

"Yes, let's," Amanda agreed, "let's fill it right up to its head, and give them a shock when they do come."

"I write to my boy friend," said Jacqueline, smiling at Elizabeth.

"You mean, you will write, or you are writing," Vanessa told her. "Her English gets no better, in fact it gets worse," she said.

The table was spread with all the things you need for writing letters, and the dolls had found the stamps from Elizabeth's post-office.

Lupin was drawing a picture.

"Lupin draws, to her friends," Vanessa explained, "I only hope they understand."

"I don't, I write in shorthand," Amanda announced. "Look, Mrs. Small, isn't it lovely, it's so quick!"

And Amanda did a whole row of hooks and eyes and dots and dashes.

"*That's* not writing, that's cheating," Vanessa said sternly.

"It isn't," Amanda argued.

"Then read me what it says at once," demanded Vanessa.

Amanda sucked her pencil.

"It says: Mrs. Small has just called," she said in triumph.

"Bless my soul, if it takes all those hooks to say that, it's not shorthand, it's longhand. The fact is, Mrs. Small, what with all the spiders' legs and the triangles and the hooks it's even more difficult to read than ABC," Vanessa explained.

Elizabeth laughed.

"It's supposed to be quicker to write," she said.

"It's simply a way of being lazy. Look at Amanda, she's done a whole page! In no time! And is it quicker to *read*? That's the point."

"He'll just make it up," Amanda said, finishing with a twirl.

"'He'! And who's he, pray?"

"The monkey, of course."

"By the way, where is Jane?" Elizabeth asked.

"Jane prefers to do hers in her room, and I don't wonder. The muddle in here is deafening," Vanessa remarked, "especially when they crumple up the ones they've done wrong."

Amanda began to fold an envelope.

"This is the best part," she said, "Jane showed us."

It was a square piece of paper.

"First you put it like a diamond," said Amanda, "with the points up and down. Then you fold the bottom point up. And then you fold the side points in, and then you get the glue," Amanda said, seizing it from Lupin, "and you glue the flap, and stick it down——"

"Look out," Elizabeth cried, "you haven't put the letter in!"

Amanda gasped.

"Just in time," she said. "I keep doing that!"

"I've sent lots of empty envelopes," Lupin confessed.

"What a *waste,* Lupin," Vanessa said in shocked tones.

"And who have you written to, Vanessa?" Elizabeth asked.

"I've written to my friend the duchess, and a great many letters about the hat business, and several invitations. And I have an old friend, Sir Clay Pipe, who's a hundred tomorrow: I'll send him a birthday card at once."

And Vanessa pulled her chair in, took some paper and chalk and began to draw. "Though I must say," she added, "that I do think it's high time we had some letters back, for all our trouble. It's very spiteful of the post people to be so slow."

"What's the difference between high time and low time?" Lupin said, sucking her pencil.

Vanessa looked very puzzled. "Really, Lupin you want to know too much! I suppose it's better than not wanting to know enough."

"It is," said Elizabeth.

"Anyway," Amanda said, "I agree with Vanessa, we shall get sick of waiting soon, and sick of doing them too," she added. "I think high time is when the clock's got his hands up, both together."

"That would be twelve o'clock," Elizabeth said.

"That's as good an explanation as any, and I hope Lupin's satisfied," Vanessa said.

Lupin threw her letter on the ground, and put her heel on it.

"There!" she said. "We've run out of stamps, now, so I'm stamping it myself."

"Excuse her ignorance, Mrs. Small," Vanessa whispered, "she doesn't know the difference between stamp and stamp, and you must say there's not much."

Elizabeth laughed, as she ran upstairs. She could see the duke in the parlour reading an empty stamp book. She knocked at Jane's door and went in.

"What are you doing?" she asked.

"I'm finishing my letters, Mrs. Small. You do think, if I post them at once in that box, they'll be delivered today, don't you?" Jane had done a good pile of letters in the neatest writing, real letters, too, with proper addresses. Elizabeth caught sight of one which said: "Lady Vanessa Crosby."

"There!" said Jane, putting down her quill. "Now I'll post them all." And she ran downstairs looking very pink and satisfied, and Elizabeth followed her. The monkey was watching Jane with solemn interest.

"That box'll be sick soon," he said. "Stuffin' it and stuffin' it them dolls are. Not good for anybody, so much paper. What's happened to the postman, anyway?"

"He's ill," Elizabeth said quickly. "If I get you a sack, can you do it for him?"

"Not 'alf," the monkey said, clambering down from the roof at once.

Elizabeth found the monkey a splendid sack. It was one which her brother had had for marbles, and was as big as he was. Then she showed him how to push aside a little door below the pillar-box mouth, to reach the letters.

The dolls were in an excited row at the dining-room window, watching.

"They're emptying the box!" squealed Lupin.

"At last!" said Jane.

"It's not a postman," said Amanda, giggling. "It's the monkey!"

"Bless my soul," screamed Vanessa. "He's simply stealing the letters!"

"It's all right," Elizabeth explained. "The post-office have sent him because the proper one's ill."

"He's not a proper one, that's certain," Vanessa sniffed. "Just look! He's got them all in the road!"

For the monkey had plunged his large fawn hand into the box, and pulled all the letters out on to the pavement. They fell in a shower, like a paper chase.

"Goodness gracious me. You don't sort them in the street! Whatever next!"

"He's muddling them not sorting them," Jane remarked. "And can he read?"

"Hush," Elizabeth said. "Let's lay the tea, while we're waiting, shall we, Vanessa?"

"A very good idea," Vanessa said, "for the more you watch things the less they happen."

This worked very well. Everybody was so busy that when the postman's knock did come, it startled them all.

Rat-a-tat-tat-tat-tat.

LETTERS

"What an impatient postman! There's no need to go on so long," Vanessa said.

"They always do," said Elizabeth.

And then the letters began coming through. First one or two. Then several at a time. Then more and more, thick and fast, whole bunches of letters.

The duke stood at the top of the stairs and said: "Lord bless me, what's this?"

"What a lot!" screamed Lupin.

"All our friends must have written at once!" Vanessa said.

But the more the letters came rustling through the more Amanda laughed. Some fat and promising, some thin and beastly, like bills. Some with beautiful addresses, but most with beautiful scribble. All the dolls rushed forward together, as it stopped raining letters, and bumped their wooden or china heads, but nobody minded.

"And I've kept a few for meself," said a gruff voice through the box in a loud whisper.

Jane and Elizabeth ran round putting a pile of letters by each plate at the table. Amanda added a few more. Lupin carefully took some from Amanda's pile and put them on her own. When the letters were shared out, each doll sat up to the table and began to open them.

"'Mrs. Coddlefish thanks Lady Crosby for

her kind invitation to tea, but is sorry not to be able to come as she has a headache,'" read Vanessa loudly. "I'm not sorry, I'm very glad, since I never asked her. What can she be thinking about?"

"She's made it up," said Lupin.

"Well, we all make things up," said Vanessa.

"And how does she know she'll have a headache when it's time to come?" asked Jane.

"She doesn't, Jane, that's the plain truth," Vanessa said nastily.

"Listen to this one: 'The Duchess of Glasstown requests the pleasure of the company of Lady Crosby and the dolls at a dance for the coming out of her daughter, Melissa,'" read Jane in her sweet voice.

"I shall borrow Jacqueline's best dress!" said Amanda.

"And what's her daughter coming out of?" asked Lupin.

"You may well ask Lupin," Vanessa said mysteriously, "and we all wonder."

"I think it means she's eighteen and counts as grown-up," Elizabeth said.

"I didn't know we knew the Duchess of Glasstown, Jane. There are plenty of duchesses I do know, but I don't recall that name. Do you, Papa?"

"Not I, my dear," said the duke, "but then

as you know I've lost my memory. In patches."

"Anyway, when is it, Jane?" Amanda said. "And where do we go?"

"It doesn't say," said Jane sadly.

"What a useless invitation," snorted Vanessa, burrowing in her pile.

"Ah. My dear friend Sir Clay Pipe says thank you for the card and he's very well and he hopes we are and he shot six pheasants and one keeper and he's coming to visit us as soon as he can get away no full stops at all," Vanessa finished breathlessly.

"Get away from what?" said Lupin.

"The keeper, no doubt," said Vanessa.

"And here's a bill for sixty-eight pounds for ice-cream," said Amanda.

"I shan't pay *that,*" Vanessa said, "for I never ate it. I only pay for what I eat."

"I've got a bill for three farthings," said Lupin.

"That will be from the bells of Saint Martin's you may be sure," Vanessa said. And she began to sing Oranges and Lemons in her high and quavery voice.

"And Hugo can't come to dinner, because he doesn't want to," said Amanda, tossing a letter away.

"How extremely rude, to be sure, but I suppose it's just as well to say what you mean," Vanessa answered.

"Anyway we never asked *him*," said Jane, "because what's the good of having someone invisible to dinner?"

"Quite so, Jane."

"Except that you wouldn't need to give them any food," said Amanda.

"Happy birthday to me," said Lupin, holding up a nice red picture.

"It's not your birthday!" shouted Amanda jealously.

"It could be," said Lupin. "Oh," she said quickly, "I've got a letter from the Queen, Vanessa!"

"Bravo, miss," said the duke.

"You never have," said Vanessa calmly. "And how is her Majesty, and what does she say?"

"She says she's very well and would we all like to go to the Palace to see her?"

"Of course we should," Vanessa said. "But when? Don't say *she's* forgotten to say when."

"She has," Lupin nodded.

"One of these days," Vanessa said, "we'll take her at her word and go."

There were lots more letters, and the cake was soon buried in them.

"I wish we had a post like this every day. But we mustn't expect it," Vanessa sighed.

"Then perhaps it'll come," added Lupin.

"Very true, Lupin. Good-bye, dear landlady,"

Vanessa said, seeing Elizabeth going. "Thank the post-office when you see it!"

"I will. Good-bye," said Elizabeth. "I've enjoyed the letters."

"So have we. Good-bye!" the dolls called.

The monkey was on the roof again, with the sack.

"Mount Pleasant up 'ere," he said, with letters all round him.

Elizabeth knew about Mount Pleasant: it is a place in London where they sort letters.

"You did keep a lot," she said. "You know you're supposed to deliver them to where they say?"

"They don't say," said the monkey wisely, "so I keeps 'em."

And he turned his back on Elizabeth and went on tossing at his pile of mail.

# VI

## APRIL FOOLS

ELIZABETH came skipping up to the dolls' house on a clear, spring day, hoping something nice would happen.

"You need to watch yer step, Mrs. Small," the monkey called from the roof.

"Why?" said Elizabeth, looking down at the path at once.

But then there was a yell from the back of the house, and Amanda came flying round, with her arms out, shrieking half with laughter and half with fright. After her came Vanessa, waving the paint brush the dolls used for a broom.

"Help, help, save me, Vanessa's coming!" yelped Amanda.

But as soon as Vanessa saw Elizabeth, she stopped dead, stood down the paint brush, and put her head on one side.

"Excuse me, dear landlady," she began breathlessly, "but *did* you know that you had four holes in your frock?"

Elizabeth looked down anxiously at the front of her dress.

"April-fool, April-fool, April-fool," screamed Amanda. "One to get in by, two for your arms and one for your head!"

And Vanessa put her hand up to her mouth and laughed for quite a long time.

Elizabeth had forgotten all about the date, as it was not a school day, but she was delighted the dolls knew.

"Who told you?" she said.

"Can't you guess?" Amanda called, running for the swing.

"The fact is, it's a ridiculous game which that monkey told Amanda, but it's simply an excuse for telling lies, as far as I can see. However, once we'd started we couldn't seem to stop, and dear Jane is counting the score to see who wins. One to me, Jane, please," called Vanessa breathlessly to Jane, who now appeared at the parlour window.

"No, ME!" said Amanda swinging.

"You did not catch Mrs. Small, I did," said Vanessa crossly.

"Hoity-toity," said the duke from the window.

"Quarrel, quarrel," jeered the monkey from the roof.

"Look out, Amanda, that rope's breaking," called Elizabeth urgently.

Amanda jumped off the swing at once.

"April-fool!" yelled Elizabeth, dancing round.

Vanessa and Jane clapped.

"Splendid, Mrs. Small, you quite have the idea, and it will do Amanda good to be caught, for a change. In fact the whole game is catching, isn't it? We can't seem to help doing it now. I really must get on, I've never been so hindered in my life. Why, Jane, here's Mrs. Small, and the beds aren't even made," she said.

"Mine is," Lupin said bouncing out.

"Good, Lupin——"

"April-fool!" yelled Lupin, jumping. "One to me, one to me, Jane."

"You see! Simply lies! It's extremely bad for everyone's behaviour," Vanessa whispered, "but we must admit it's very amusing and different."

"You drop your pen, Jane," said Jacqueline.

"Do I, I mean have I?" said Jane puzzled.

"April fish!" squealed the paying-guest, as they say it in France.

"Fish, indeed!" said Vanessa. "Trust the French to think out some ridiculous word, just to be different."

"One to Jacqueline," wrote Jane. "Vanessa, that kettle you put on's boiling over," she said.

"Oh!" shrieked Vanessa, holding on her hat, and diving for the door.

"April-fool!" called Jane softly, going very pink. "One to me at last," she added.

"Is that your first?" said Elizabeth.

"Yes, because I'm so busy keeping this score, you see, I haven't had time to think any out," explained Jane.

"Come in at once, you dolls," called Vanessa's voice from the house, "because there's a drink for you."

Everybody dashed into the house, and Jane ran downstairs.

"April-fools!" sang Vanessa triumphantly.

"Six to me, Jane, all in one fell swoop! Splendid, I should think I've certainly won."

"Oh, Vanessa, what a mean one," wailed Amanda.

"Not six, Vanessa, five," Jane said, as she counted them.

"What about me? I didn't get a drink, either, did I?" Vanessa said.

"You can't fool *yourself*," Elizabeth protested. "Five, Jane."

"Very well, as you say, but you seem rather fond of making rules, Mrs. Small," sniffed Vanessa. "When they suit you. Now, Jane and I will finish the beds. Lupin, you are to dust round the duke in the parlour, the paying-guest is to polish the dining-room table. Do you comprehend?" said Vanessa. "Polish, rub, shine, the table in there, until you can see your face," Vanessa said. "Not that anybody would want to see your face," she muttered under her breath. "Nobody is to hinder me any more with this nonsense, I declare the game over," she ended.

"That's because you think you've won," Amanda said cheekily. "I declare it still on." And she ran upstairs after Lupin to the parlour, where they at once began having a cushion fight.

"Oh, mind the duke, mind the duke!" Vanessa said, as a cushion flew past his Grace's left ear.

"Lupin, don't be so trying," she called.

"But you always say try, try, try again," answered Lupin.

"That's another *kind* of trying," snapped Vanessa. "Ask Papa to explain."

"Vanessa!" shouted Elizabeth, up the stairs, "I was just tidying the hall, when a letter came through your letter-box!"

"No!" began Vanessa smiling and turning round. "I don't believe you," she added quickly, "you can't fool me."

"I'm not. Here it is. Look. It's not really a letter, it's a card."

"Read it, read it!"

All the dolls gathered on the upstairs landing, the duke included.

"You are all very easily caught," Vanessa sniffed. "Any letter that comes today, must be an April-fool letter, Mrs. Small ought to throw it straight on the fire. You can't catch us," Vanessa shouted to the world at large very loudly.

"Well, what does it say?" asked Jane. "It may be funny."

"Or it may be money," Amanda added.

"Not on a postcard," Elizabeth said. "It says:

'Hugo. Cort Fertograffer.
Takes her Majesty.

Will call this morning and take
a free pawtrate.
No obbligashun to by.'"

There was complete silence for a minute, and then the dolls began to talk.

"Hugo!" said Jane. "Perhaps that's the monkey's invisible friend!"

"Anything to do with the monkey is bound to be an April-fool, I warn you," Vanessa said. "Caught photographer, indeed. We don't mind as long as he's caught, and not us——"

"It doesn't mean *that* caught, Vanessa, it's spelt the other way, it means the Queen's Court," explained Elizabeth.

"The Queen certainly is NOT caught," Vanessa argued, "nobody would dare to do it, they'd have their heads cut off!"

"They've only got one head," put in Lupin.

"Also, 'Takes the Queen,' " Vanessa added. "Takes her *where,* pray? I never heard such nonsense."

"It means this Hugo goes to the Court and takes her photo——" Elizabeth said, laughing.

"And now he's coming here to take ours!" finished Jane, clapping her hands.

"Free!" put in the duke. "Well upon my word what more do you want?"

"It'll be no good if it's free," Vanessa snapped.

"The last line's the best," Amanda said. "It doesn't mean a single thing. Read it again, Mrs. Small."

" 'No obbligashun to by,' " read Elizabeth. "It's the spelling that's so funny——"

"You can't have to and by together, I agree with Amanda," Vanessa said, "you might as well say from with. And what on earth does that obble word mean, pray?"

"I think it means he comes and takes the portrait, but we don't have to buy it if we don't like it. He's spelt buy wrong, that's all."

"Well, we all make mistakes. But he can't be a very good photographer if he can't spell buy."

"He can't spell anything," Jane said, looking at the card. "But then you don't have to spell to take photos, do you?"

"Certainly not," said his Grace.

"Perhaps it's because he's invisible?" Lupin suggested, "and can't see what he's saying."

"You've got invisible the wrong way round," said Elizabeth. "It's we who can't see *him.*"

"I say," began Amanda, "how do we know when he comes if he's invisible?"

"Precisely!" Vanessa said. "Amanda is very quick-witted and clever today, it must be the April-fooling. How do we know, Papa?" she demanded.

The duke scratched his head.

"Perhaps he'll just speak," said Elizabeth at last.

"Oooh!" Lupin shuddered.

"How ghostly," whispered Jane.

"Let's not have him," said Amanda.

"If he says he's coming, and we can't see him, we can't stop him," said Elizabeth.

"So we'd better make the best of it," Vanessa said briskly. "All dress up nicely. Comb your hair, Lupin (or your wool, I should say) . Jane, polish your face, and brush Papa's coat. Amanda, put on your brooch, the paying-guest isn't invited, and the rest you can think out for yourselves."

And Vanessa darted into her room to put on more rouge. Soon the dolls were all gathered in the hall, and Lupin was watching the door nervously.

"Will it open when he comes in?" she asked.

"I think he's here," Amanda stated. "He's black. He's on the back lawn."

"If he's black, he's not invisible," Vanessa said. "You can't be both," and she led the way to one of the back windows to look.

There was a black tent on the green velvet, which Elizabeth could see had been made out of the deck-chairs and a curtain. Inside it was a stool, and on the stool stood her tiny toy camera.

"That's it!" she said. "I can see the camera. And they always go under a kind of black tent affair. It's because they have to be in the dark, I think."

"In the dark, and invisible, what very cunning people they must be! Is it safe to go out?" said Vanessa. But she went all the same.

"Good-morning, photographer," she said, nodding bravely at the empty tent. "I hope you left her Majesty well?"

There was no answer.

"Now, all sit in a clump, here in front," Elizabeth told them, wondering very much what would happen.

"Clump, Mrs. Small? We're not flowers, except for Lupin. Fetch the kitten, Lupin. Oh, and a chair for Papa."

When everybody was at last collected, Robin in Jane's arms, the kitten in Lupin's, and the duke in his chair, Elizabeth said:

"Now, you all have to look at the camera, and say 'cheese.' "

"Why cheese?"

"Because it makes you smile."

"It doesn't make me smile, I hate it," Lupin said, with feeling.

"Don't argue, Lupin."

"Then say please," Elizabeth suggested. "When I say go, altogether. Ready, steady——"

"Just like sports day," said Amanda.

"Be quiet, Amanda," Vanessa said sharply.

"Ready, steady, go," said Elizabeth.

"CHEESE," said all the dolls together.

There was a faint click from the camera, and up sprang the jack-in-a-box who always came out when you moved the switch. He was a little black jack.

The duke said, "Ha!" Lupin jumped, Amanda shrieked with laughter, Vanessa looked very surprised and cross, and Jane comforted Robin.

"It's all right, it always does that," Elizabeth said quickly, "I expect it's to make you smile. Thank you, Hugo," she said getting up.

Lupin and Amanda rushed at once to see the jack-in-a-box.

"Thank you indeed," added Vanessa, "and where is the photo, may we ask? Or is that invisible too?"

"Oh, Vanessa, you never have the photo at once," Elizabeth explained. "You have to wait days, while they develop and print it."

"It sounds like measles," Vanessa sniffed. "I told you so. No photo. The whole thing is an April-fool, Papa, and I was the only one who knew it, so it's six, no seven, no eight to me. Nine counting the caught photographer."

"Oh, Vanessa!"

"It's a dear little man," Lupin said.

"Come along, dinner-time, it was pleasant to dress up, anyway, dear landlady," sang Vanessa, "and we'll believe in that photo when we see it." And she took the duke's arm to go in.

"Good-bye," Elizabeth called. "It's high time I went."

"Good-bye, we have enjoyed April-fools," whispered Jane, turning round to wave.

"Monkey, how did you move the switch?" Elizabeth said, when all the dolls were safely inside.

"Hugo moved it. He was in that tent."

"But he's not really there," said Elizabeth.

"He is. I've made him up. You have to make people up for when you're lonely," the monkey explained.

This was very true, and Elizabeth knew it. She waved at him extra hard as she walked away.

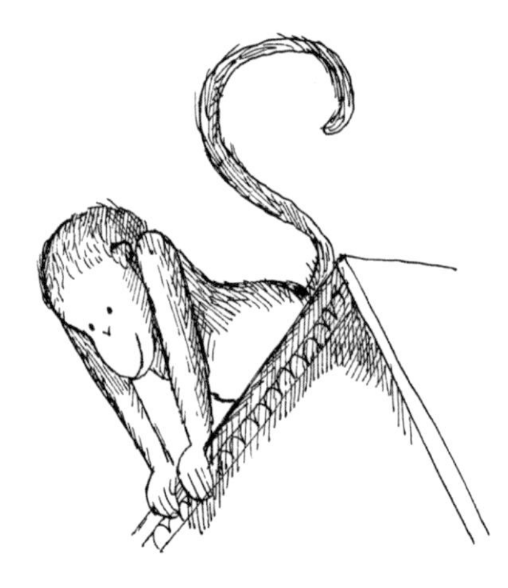

# VII

## THE THEATRE

THE time had come to return the Duke of Cranberry. Elizabeth was wondering how she could manage this, when she saw that his sedan-chair was already in the front. As she knocked at the door the monkey called out:

" 'is Grace is going!"

"How do you know?" she said.

" 'ow does he know, that's the question," said the monkey, winking. "Mrs. Small, who's going to carry 'is chair?"

"The men who brought it, I expect."

"Well, can me and Hugo? I'd like to go to Cranberry Castle. It would be a nice change. And I likes the old duke, too."

But just then Lupin and Amanda ran to open the door.

"Mrs. Small," they said together, "the duke's going tonight! Come upstairs, we're all in the parlour."

"Good afternoon, dear Mrs. Small," Vanessa said. Her voice was a little tearful and she dabbed at her eyes with one of the duke's new handkerchiefs. "Excuse my tears, I don't often do it——"

"I've never seen you before," Elizabeth agreed in surprise.

"But dear Papa says he must go——"

The duke was standing by the painted table, tapping his fingers upon it.

"Now come, come, daughter," he said briskly, "no tears, or your paint will run." This was very true. "I'm excessively glad to see you, Ma'am," he said to Elizabeth, "for you will know the neighbourhood. I intend to take the ladies to the theatre, as it is the last day of my visit. May I entrust you with the purchase of the tickets?"

Elizabeth opened her mouth in surprise and then gazed from the duke to Vanessa.

"Papa, dear," Vanessa began, drying her tears, "I was thinking, what about a trip to the Zoo?"

The duke frowned and walked over to the window.

"For at least we know it's there," went on Vanessa to Elizabeth in a loud whisper, behind her hand.

"What!" barked the duke, "take you all in your fine clothes to look at a lot of smelly animals——"

"Oh, but they're not smelly," said Jane sweetly.

"*All* animals are smelly," the duke said, "present company excepted," he called up the chimney. He had got used to the idea of the monkey on the roof. "No, I want to take you to the theatre. Why on earth not?"

Vanessa looked helplessly at Elizabeth. "Dearest Papa," she said, bravely, "the plain fact is, that we don't think there *is* a theatre, anywhere within miles!"

"Heyday!" said the duke. "What a melancholy state of affairs. Mrs. Small, Ma'am, I feel sure you know of a theatre?"

Elizabeth's cheeks were as pink as Vanessa's with excitement, wondering. "I do," she said.

"But I'm not sure if there will be a play on when you want it!"

"Oh! Mrs. Small!"

All the young dolls shrieked with delight and rushed at Elizabeth. As for Vanessa, she went over and took her Papa's arm, and together they did a few steps of the duke's dance, looking as gay and perky as two robins.

"Bravo, bravo!" said the duke. "And here's a sovereign for the tickets," he added, putting a golden guinea into Elizabeth's hand.

"Now, everybody get dressed," Vanessa said. "Papa is going straight home after the theatre, Mrs. Small, and it's very easy getting *him* ready, as he has absolutely no luggage."

"But I think he ought to have some food for the journey," said Jane, "so I've put some rent in a packet," she whispered, "in his pocket."

"In a packet in his pocket, in a packet in his pocket," sang Amanda running upstairs after Lupin.

The little theatre was a model one Edward had made last Christmas. Elizabeth had sewed the red velvet curtains, and cut out the cardboard figures for the plays. Cinderella was the best, she decided. She put the kitchen scene and Cinderella herself, ready. She switched on the two little torches Edward had arranged at each side as footlights. She thought that she could manage to push the figures on, and change the scenery and tell the story, but what Vanessa would say she could not think. Also she would think it very strange if they had to bring their own chairs, or sit on the floor. So Elizabeth scuttled to her cupboard and pushed across a square cardboard egg tray which she had painted crimson. There were rows of holes where the eggs sat, and between the holes were points. However, along the edge there was a little space between each point where a doll might balance. They were strange theatre seats, but better than a large piece of empty floor.

When she got back, everybody was ready in the front garden. The duke was in his chair, and the monkey stood between the back poles. Elizabeth picked up the front poles and led the way. The rest followed in the mouse-and-trap.

"Here we are," she said, stopping before the theatre, near to the crimson seats.

Vanessa looked very surprised. "What a very strange theatre to be sure," she whispered. "It's more like a Punch and Judy show, Mrs. Small, in the street like this." And she jumped down, and ran to help the duke.

"Ha!" said he. "Now the tickets?"

"You don't need tickets," Elizabeth said,

"because it is a special performance for the duke."

"How very genteel," replied Vanessa, forgiving the theatre at once for being in the street.

"Are these the seats?" called Amanda.

"That's it, in front. You must sit on the little ledge between the holes," Elizabeth explained.

"I'm not, I'm the king of the castle," screamed Amanda on top of a crimson point.

"I'm going to sit in a hole," shrieked Lupin, jumping into one.

"You won't be able to see," Jane said, sedately leading the duke to a ledge, and then perching upon another.

"Bless my soul," Vanessa said, "I should think these seats were made for very large, round, egg-shaped people, like Humpty-Dumpty you know. Just look at that lazy monkey!"

For the monkey had sat back into a hole, with his fawn feet stuck out in front.

"Let him do as he likes," said the duke, who now got on with the monkey very well.

"Look at the curtains," Lupin said. "I love the colour. Can I draw them back? Who draws them back?"

"Nobody knows," Vanessa said wisely, "it's magic."

"If everybody will stop chattering," said the duke, "no doubt the play will begin. You cannot expect the curtains to open if you are not ready. Now, Ma'am," he said to Elizabeth, as a complete silence fell over the audience, "what is the piece, did you say?"

"Cinderella," said Elizabeth anxiously. And then a lovely and surprising thing happened. The crimson curtains began slowly and quietly to open.

"Good!" breathed Lupin.

There was the big fireplace, and sad, pretty Cinderella sitting by it. There was her broom. There were the pots and pans, the table, the benches, the stools and the clock on the wall.

"There's Cinders," said Amanda.

"She's rather like Jane," said Lupin.

And the play began. Cinderella got up from the fireplace to sweep the floor. The Ugly Sisters came striding in and their voices were as scratchy as slate pencils, as they bullied Cinderella.

"Cinders! Fetch my shoes!"

"Cinders, chop up this wood!"

"Cinderella! Bring in the coals. Peel the potatoes. Go and make the beds!"

"Bless my soul," whispered Vanessa, "I never saw such thin actresses in all my life. They're wasting away!"

This was not surprising, as they were made of cardboard.

"They've got thin voices, too," said Lupin.

"Oh, hush, they're beating Cinderella!" said Jane.

"Why doesn't she hit them back?" said Lupin, standing up.

"She should take that frying-pan, and bash them on the head. I would, wouldn't you, Lupin?" Amanda said.

"Yes, and I'd trip them up and I'd pinch them and I'd put things in their beds, and——"

"Hush," said Jane, "I can't hear, and it's so exciting."

Jacqueline sat perched on her crimson point, watching with wide eyes.

"Yes, hush, indeed," said Vanessa. "Though of course we know what happens."

"Yes, but we want to know again," explained Jane. And Elizabeth agreed.

"Lupin, sit *down*," Vanessa hissed. "The people behind you won't be able to see."

"There aren't any people behind me," said Lupin, looking at the empty holes.

"You never know who there may be behind you," said Vanessa.

"Listen!" Amanda said.

There was a tiny fanfare of trumpets, and in came the messenger from the King.

"Oh, look at his buckles!"

"I like his rosettes."

The old father bowed and scraped before the messenger, and showed off his ugly daughters, who simpered and swayed their heads and spread out their skirts.

"They think they're pretty," Lupin announced loudly, "but they're jolly well not."

All the young ladies in the land were to go to the palace, and from amongst them the prince would choose his bride. The Ugly Sisters ran off to get ready, and Cinders sat sadly by the fire again.

Lupin scrambled off her seat as the crimson curtains began to close.

"You should let her go," she shouted angrily at the old father. "You should let Cinderella go to the ball!"

"Oh, hush, Lupin," Vanessa said, pulling her back, "you never speak to the actors, they're in another world, in the story."

"But I want to be in the story, Vanessa," Lupin explained. "Can I get into the story if I climb on the stage?"

"What a suggestion," Vanessa said. "Watch, look, it's starting again."

"It's those old sisters!"

"In their bedroom!"

"Look, they're putting on rouge. Like Vanessa! Like you do, Vanessa."

"They're putting on far too *much*," Vanessa said sternly.

"They're putting on more hair too."

"You girls are much too talkative," said the duke. "I can't hear."

"Nor can I," Jane added.

"*I* want to be an actress," Amanda decided. "How do they know what to say, Mrs. Small?"

"They learn it off by heart," said Elizabeth.

"All *that*. They never could. I should just make it up," she said.

And so the play went on. When the sisters went to the ball, Amanda hissed and Lupin booed. But when the Fairy Godmother and the pumpkin coach came! "Oh!" they said. "This is the best part!" And they crept to the foot of the stage and stared at the coach with round eyes.

And Jane stood up and clasped her hands.

And Vanessa said, "Bless me!" very softly.

And Jacqueline said, *"Ciel!"*

And the duke said, "Only look!"

And the monkey scrambled up out of his egg-hole and cheered, in a stage whisper.

Then Cinderella came forward in her lovely dress, stepped into the coach, and went to the ball.

"Oh, Vanessa, I wish I could go to the ball!" sighed Lupin.

"Look, watch, here she is," said Jane.

"There's the prince. He's seen her. He likes her doesn't he?" Lupin said.

"That he does," said the duke.

"He's dancing with her."

"He's not dancing with those old sisters at all."

"Mrs. Small, it's high time, isn't it?" Amanda said. "Look at the clock, it's got its arms up!"

The clock struck twelve.

"Quick, Cinderella!"

"Run, run Cinders," Lupin squealed, jumping up and down.

"There she goes!"

"There goes her shoe, her glass slipper," said Jane.

"Now she's all rags again, isn't she?" Amanda said as the curtains closed.

"Rags and tatters," said Vanessa, sadly.

"Rags and tatters, tags and ratters," said Amanda. "Come on, hurry," she urged the closed curtain.

But perhaps the best scene of all was when the prince came with the glass slipper on a cushion, searching for the mysterious princess.

The first Ugly Sister's foot was much too long.

And the second Ugly Sister's foot was much too fat.

"Boo," said Amanda. "Serves you right."

"Let Cinderella try," demanded Lupin.

"Come on, Cinderella! Good old Cinders!" they yelled.

And Jane stood up again with shining eyes to watch the slipper go on.

"Hooray!" shouted the dolls. "Bravo!" added the duke.

"It fits her, she's won, hasn't she, Vanessa?"

"What's she won?" Lupin whispered.

"The prince!" said Jane. "Happily ever after."

When the crimson curtains closed for the last time, the dolls clapped and cheered and waved, as if they would never stop, and Vanessa lost her balance clapping and fell into an egg-hole.

"No harm done," she sang, scrambling out again. "It's these ridiculous holes. I should think they were meant for toads. Stop stamping at once, Monkey, it's most vulgar!"

"It's not me, it's Hugo," he said breathlessly.

"Mrs. Small, what happens to them when the play's over?" Lupin said.

"Are they hiding behind the curtain still?" asked Amanda. "Can I peep?"

"Certainly not," Vanessa said. "It isn't a peep-show. A delightful play," she went on, "and a splendid audience." And she looked back over the rows of empty holes. "All invisible," she added, "like Hugo."

"Now, my dears," began the old Duke of

Cranberry, "let me see you in and safely off, before I start my journey." And he trotted up to Vanessa, took her arm and led her to the trap.

"Oh, Papa," she wailed, "I'd forgotten. I'd forgotten you were going!"

"Then I heartily advise you to forget again," he said. "I can forget things whenever I want to, and it's most useful."

This seemed an excellent idea, and the dolls piled into the trap in high spirits, each kissing the duke in turn.

"Good-bye, Duke, good-bye, good-bye!" they called.

"*Au revoir,*" called Jacqueline.

"Come again," said Jane.

"Thank you for the theatre," added Elizabeth, who was going with them.

"Thank *you,* Ma'am," said he bowing.

And they saw him step into the sedan-chair, and the monkey, standing to attention beside it. They waved till they were almost home.

"Oh, I wish I were in a play, Vanessa, I wish I could be," Lupin sighed as they arrived.

"Why perhaps we're all in a play, Lupin, who knows? I often wonder why I'm Vanessa. Perhaps people like it."

"They do," said Elizabeth at once, without having to think. "They like you all being you."

"That's as good a reason as you could find, for

being us," said Vanessa. "Bedtime!" she sang, as they trooped into the dolls' house. "Up we go. Hurry, Lupin. Careful, Amanda. *Vite, vite,* Jacqueline. Mind your dress, Jane. Good-bye dear, dear Mrs. Small, we did enjoy the play."

"Oh, we did," said Jane, squeezing Elizabeth's arm. "It's the best thing we've ever done!"

"Nearly," said Amanda.

"Quite," added Lupin.

"Good-night! I hope dear Papa's safe. He seems to trust that monkey."

"Good-night! Good-bye!" Elizabeth called, as they closed the door. And she stayed for a long while watching through the windows, as the lights went on all over the house. There was Vanessa, back in her four-poster bed. And Jane, undoing Jacqueline's dress. And Jacqueline with her mouth full of rent. And Lupin and Amanda bouncing and bouncing on Lupin's cushions on the floor.

Elizabeth waited until the lights went out, and a gruff, sleepy voice above her said:

"Got 'is Grace back safely, Mrs. Small."

"Oh, Monkey, I thought you were going to stay!" Elizabeth answered.

"No. . . . I missed my roof," said he, curling round into a ball to go to sleep.

THE END

The book you have read was first published in England. You may have noticed that the English spelling of some words is different from the American. The English, for example, spell color with a "u"—colour. The English meanings of words and phrases are sometimes different from ours as well. Below you will find the American meaning of some words and phrases in this book that may puzzle you.

# GLOSSARY

*Busby:* Tall fur hat worn by soldiers of some British regiments

*Cheeky:* Fresh, bold

*Cravat:* Large frilled tie

*Dustman:* Garbageman

*Fender:* Curb surrounding an open fire hearth

*Peep-show:* A small scene in a box, viewed through a little hole

*Pillar-box:* Rural mail box

*Scrum:* A pushing crowd

*Trap:* A kind of buggy

HELEN CLARE is the pen name of Pauline Clarke, the well-known English author. She has written many books for children under both names.

Her book *The Twelve and the Genii,* won the 1962 Carnegie Award in England. It is called *The Return of the Twelves* in its American edition.